JoJo & GranGran

This JoJo & Gran Gran
storybook belongs to:

_____

First published in Great Britain in 2021 by Pat-a-Cake
Pat-a-Cake is a registered trademark of Hodder & Stoughton Limited
This book copyright © BBC 2021
JoJo & Gran Gran and the CBeebies logo are trademarks of the British Broadcasting Corporation and are used under licence
Based on original characters by Laura Henry-Allain
Additional images © Shutterstock
ISBN 978 1 52638 335 8
1 3 5 7 9 10 8 6 4 2
Pat-a-Cake, an imprint of Hachette Children's Group,
Part of Hodder & Stoughton Limited
Carmelite House, 50 Victoria Embankment, London EC4Y 0DZ
An Hachette UK Company
www.hachette.co.uk - www.hachettechildrens.co.uk
Printed and bound in China
A CIP catalogue record for this book is available from the British Library

JoJo & Gran Gran

VISIT THE FARM

pat a cake

Picture Glossary

Here are some words from JoJo's visit to the farm.

JoJo

Gran Gran

Julie

sheep

llama

goat

hatchery

egg

chick

chickens

It was a spring morning, the blossom was on the trees, the sun was shining and JoJo and Gran Gran were on their way to the farm.

JoJo was very excited.

"Gran Gran, I can't wait to show you Melanie. She's my favourite chick at the farm," said JoJo.

"I can't wait to meet her," smiled Gran Gran.

"Look, here's a picture of me with Mummy, Daddy and Melanie!" cried JoJo excitedly. "She's so tiny, fluffy and yellow!"

"Hmmm, Melanie might not be quite so tiny anymore, JoJo. You haven't been to the farm in a while, have you?" asked Gran Gran.

"It wasn't that long ago," said JoJo.

Soon, JoJo and Gran Gran arrived at the farm. A friendly farmer in wellies came up to them.

"Hello there! Welcome to the City Farm. I'm Julie," she smiled. "If you need to know anything about our animals, just ask me," she said.

"Hello, I'm JoJo."

"Nice to meet you, JoJo. Have you visited the farm before?" asked Julie.

"Oh yes," said JoJo excitedly. "I came with my Mummy and Daddy . . . and now I want to show Gran Gran all the animals that I saw!"

"Well, they're all still here, JoJo," replied Julie.

JoJo's eyes lit up. "Even Melanie?" she asked.

"Even Melanie," Julie nodded.

"Yay!" shouted JoJo.

JoJo ran towards the first pen.

"Look, Gran Gran! Here are the sheep!"

"I can see that, JoJo," laughed Gran Gran.

"Hello, sheep. Do you remember me?" asked JoJo.

"Baaaa!" said the sheep.

"Baaaa, baaaa," replied JoJo!

JoJo jumped up and down in excitement. Gran Gran took out her tablet to take a photo.

"Say cheese!"

"Cheeeese!" yelled JoJo.

"Baaaa!" bleated the sheep.

After saying goodbye to the sheep, JoJo and Gran Gran made their way to the goat pen. There was a grey goat with a long beard and two big horns on its head.

"Look, Gran Gran!" said JoJo. "This is Nanny the nanny goat. Last time we came to the farm she tried to nibble Daddy's jacket! Hello Nanny, do you remember me?"

"Meeh!" cried the nanny goat.

"Meeh, meeh!" replied JoJo.

Gran Gran pulled out her tablet,

"Say cheese!"

"Cheeeese!" yelled JoJo.

"Meeh!" cried the goat.

As JoJo was smiling for the photo, the
nanny goat started to nibble her coat, too.

"Nooooo, Nanny! I'm not straw!" giggled JoJo.

Then JoJo and Gran Gran visited the next pen.

"This is Luna, she's a . . . a . . ." JoJo tried to remember what Luna was.

"Llama. Luna is a llama," said Gran Gran.

"Yes, that's right! She's a llama!"

Gran Gran read the information on the side of the pen. "It says here that Luna is four years old."

"Hello Luna, do you remember me?" asked JoJo.

Gran Gran took a selfie of all three of them. "Say cheese!"

"Cheeeese!" yelled JoJo and Gran Gran.

"Mmmmm!" hummed the llama.

"Who's next, JoJo?" asked Gran Gran.

"Ummmmmm, Melanieeeeeeee!" shouted JoJo as she ran ahead excitedly.

JoJo held out her picture and raced up to the chicken run to look
through the fence.

"Melanie?" called JoJo as she stood on her tiptoes,
looking over the fence.

JoJo looked this way and that, then ran around to
the other side. "Mel-a-nie, where arrrrrre yooooou?"
But all JoJo could see were grown-up chickens.

"Gran Gran, I can't see Melanie anywhere!" JoJo sighed sadly.
"Hmm . . . JoJo, I think it's time for a Gran Gran Plan.
Let's ask Julie!"

Julie was in the pen feeding the chickens. "How can I help, JoJo?"
"I can't find Melanie!" said JoJo as she looked at the photo of the
tiny yellow chick.

"Well, Melanie IS here! But she's grown up quite a lot since you last saw her. Do you see that chicken there?" asked Julie.

JoJo looked over towards the chicken.

"Y-e-s . . . " replied JoJo slowly.

"Well, that's Melanie!"

JoJo giggled, "No, it's not!"

JoJo looked at the chicken, then looked at her photo. And then looked at the chicken again.

Julie walked over to Melanie.

"Melanie, shall we show JoJo how quickly chickens grow up?"

"Cluck, cluck!" replied Melanie.

Julie took JoJo and Gran Gran to look at a special chart.

"Melanie hatched from an egg. At first she was a tiny, fluffy, yellow chick," explained Julie.

"That's when you first met her, JoJo," said Gran Gran.

"Ah . . . " sighed JoJo.

"Then, Melanie started to grow bigger and bigger, and grow more and more brown feathers!"

"Woah!" said JoJo.

"Until she became the grown-up chicken she is today!"

JoJo looked at Melanie curiously. "But I haven't grown that much."

"Well, some animals grow more quickly than people," said Gran Gran.

"You can give her a little stroke if you like," said Julie.

JoJo walked slowly up to Melanie, trying not to scare her.

"Hello, Melanie . . . you're a grown-up chicken now," whispered JoJo.

"Cluck, cluck!" replied Melanie.

"She's still really soft, Gran Gran!"

"Would you like a new photo with Melanie?" asked Julie.

"Yes, please!" said JoJo.

"Do you want to see where we keep some of the eggs?" asked Julie.

"Oooooh, yes please!" squeaked JoJo.

"This building is called a hatchery. It's a very special place. When we go inside we have to be VERY quiet, okay?" explained Julie.

"Okay!" whispered JoJo.

"Okay!" whispered Gran Gran.

Inside, the hatchery looked really cosy. Looking around, they could see it was full of eggs.

"This is an incubator. We keep the eggs safe and warm in here until they're ready to hatch."

JoJo looked very carefully at all the eggs. As she watched, one of them started to move.

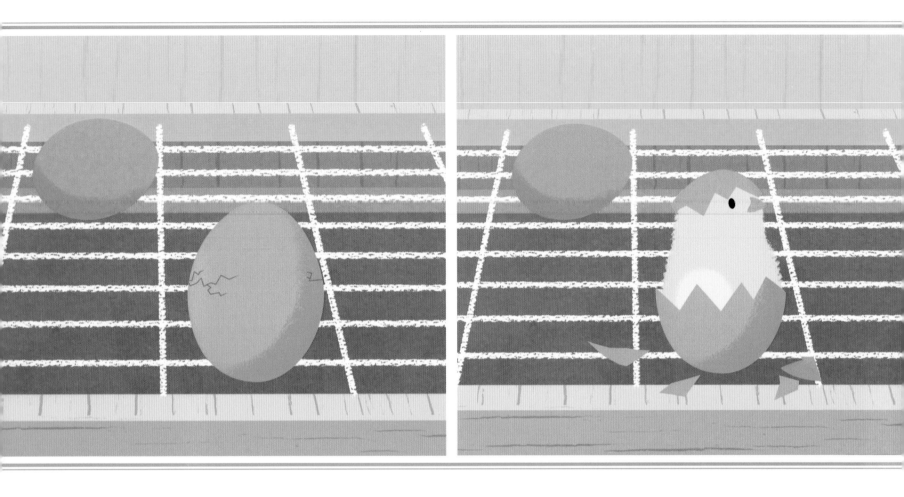

The small egg began to rumble and wobble, it teetered and
tottered and then . . . crack!

"Ohhhh!" JoJo gasped.

"Look, JoJo!" cried Gran Gran.

The egg had cracked and a tiny, fluffy, yellow head appeared.

"Cheep, cheep!" chirped the chick.

"Awwwww. Wow. She's so tiny, fluffy and yellow," whispered JoJo.

"Would you like to name her?" chuckled Julie.

"Yes please! I'd like to call her . . . um . . . M . . . Margery!" said JoJo proudly.

"Cheep, cheep!" chirped Margery.

When JoJo and Gran Gran got home, they looked at all the photos from their visit to the farm.

"Thank you for taking me to the farm," said JoJo. "Maybe next time we go, Margery will be as big as Melanie!"

"Maybe!" replied Gran Gran.

"Cluck, cluck!" chirped JoJo, flapping her arms.

"Cluck, cluck!" replied Gran Gran.

"I love you, Gran Gran," said JoJo as they snuggled up.

"Ahh, I love you too, JoJo!"

Animal Noises

JoJo had lots of fun practising her animal noises at the farm.
How many animal noises can you make?

Can you chirp
like a chick?

"Cheep, cheep!"

Can you baa
like a sheep?

"Baaaa!"

Can you bleat
like a goat?

"Meeeeh, meeeh!"

Can you cluck
like a chicken?

"Cluck, cluck!"